Bob Moats

Stoney Hawk

By Bob Moats

For information and address:
Magic 1 Productions
P.O. Box 524, Fraser MI 48026-0524
Website: http://murdernovels.com
Cover by Bob Moats

Bob Moats

Extra special thanks to:

Special thanks to Susan Haughton, who edited this book and for her great suggestions.

Thanks to the beta readers Cindy Valstad, Al Norris, Amy Morningstar. Thanks to Russ Holthaus for his experience in law enforcement for checking police procedures.

Thank you to all the people who purchased this book. I hope you enjoy it as much as I enjoyed writing it for my faithful readers.

The Jim Richards Family of Readers is listed in the back of the book.

'Stoney End' from The Essential Barbra Streisand 1971
Songwriter, Laura Nyro
Lyrics Published by © Sony/ATV Music Publishing LLC

~~*~~

Chapter 1

"I was born from love and my poor mother worked the mines
I was raised on the good book Jesus
Till I read between the lines
Now I don't believe I want to see the morning."

The Barbra Streisand song, "*Stoney End*" played on the car radio and Stoney thought of her mother. She never worked the mines, but her job working in a laundry of a hotel was just as bad. Stoney was born from a quickie union between a man and her mother, and in 1972, she was born. Her father left before he even knew about her mother's pregnancy and all these years Stoney wondered who he was. Her mother refused to say, or she didn't know, so Stoney pretended that he was some big name rock star her mother had gotten together with in the band's bus after his show.

Her mother loved this song so when she was born, she became Stoney. She was glad her favorite song wasn't *'Jeremiah was a Bullfrog.'* Her mother died two years ago and even on her deathbed refused to tell her who her father was. She reached over and spun the volume dial to ear-bleeding loud and sang along.

She thought the biggest reason she got into private investigating was because she wanted to solve the mystery of who her old man was. Her real name was Stoney Iskowitz, but luckily her mother married and she took his last name, Hawk. She liked the sound of Stoney Hawk, it sounded tough and dangerous, which is what she trained herself to be. She grew up in a bad area of Detroit, a place where you fought almost every day to survive. As a girl growing up there, she fought the best of the punks who inhabited the neighborhood and after a while they left her alone.

After high school, having a reputation for being the bad girl, she joined the Army. She survived basic training and took the taunts and threats from the other maggots. After basic she was assigned a desk job in the headquarters for the Army Special Forces. She would watch the men training and made a few friends who took her in and taught her their expertise in combat and black ops. She left the Army when her hitch ended and went on a quest to find her father.

She found out from an old P.I. in Detroit that she could get more information by having a license to investigate. So she went to a local community college, took the classes and eventually got her license. She was now officially a private investigator.

She went to work for a while on her own and still had no luck finding anything about her father. Her mother never kept records or a diary about her life. The father's name part of her birth certificate was left blank, so was her heart. She finally gave up and concentrated on her new profession. She took numerous classes in martial arts and Krav Maga. She would hit the gym and work out, being hit on by a number of pumped up numbskulls. She never married, although she had one close brush with a cop named Doyle. They lasted for about a half year, but he wasn't interested in marriage. He lost his wife in a car accident, and couldn't let go of her memory. Stoney left him and struck out to work her profession and got busy fairly fast.

She drove out to Eastpointe to where she was to meet with a new client. The woman was having problems with her ex-boyfriend and wanted him out of her life. Stoney was doing protection occasionally and equalizing problem cases. She usually could convince a trouble making ex-spouse or misguided boyfriend to back off.

She drove into the parking lot of the Cloverleaf Restaurant at Gratiot and Nine Mile Road. She didn't know what the woman looked like but Stoney had described herself. Curly blond hair down to her waist and tall. She always wore a spandex jumpsuit, it was easy to move in when she had to move fast. She may have looked like a hooker most of the time, but it was useful the rest of the time.

Stoney entered the place and saw a woman alone in a booth waving to her. She went to the woman and sat.

"Marcy?" she asked. The woman said she was. "I'm Stoney Hawk, what can I do for you?" Stoney knew what she wanted, but she wanted her to say the words aloud.

"My ex-boyfriend is bothering me, threatening me. I want him gone. The police can't do anything. I'd have to be beaten to a pulp before they could stop him and it would be only temporary. I'm afraid to even leave my house." She looked on the verge of tears.

"Did you bring the photo I asked for?"

She nodded her head and took a photo out of an envelope and handed it to Stoney. "His name is Brian Estes."

Stoney looked at the man and said, "This is a good shot. Thanks."

"What's your fee, Miss Hawk?"

"For domestic violence cases, I charge nothing. I'm just glad to make the world a little safer from the scum. When was the last time you saw him?"

"Late last night, he was out front of my house honking his horn. Then he spray painted my garage door, it said slut." Now she started crying softly.

"Has he ever beaten you?"

"Yes, a number of times," she said wiping her eyes with a napkin. "I ended up in the hospital twice and the police still couldn't do much. He was arrested but he was released the next day after posting a small bail."

"How often do you see him?"

"Almost every day now. He just won't quit."

"Well, I have some friends who may want to talk to him, so I'll take care of it. Give me a few days. If you see him, or me, out front of your house, just stay in."

"Thank you, Miss Hawk. I don't know where else to go. I'm glad I found your ad in the paper. It's good to know there are people who care."

"No problem, go home and rest. I'll call when this is settled," Stoney said and stood. She left the restaurant and drove back to her office in Detroit. She was in the process of moving it to Sterling Heights. She had gotten tired of the city.

She went into the building and checked her phone messages. Nothing of importance, so she sat and thought about her ad. She grew up watching an 80's TV show called the *Equalizer*, with British actor Edward Woodward. She loved watching him solve people's problems the same way she would handle Brian Estes. His name was Robert McCall, an unaffiliated private eye, and he always put an ad in the paper for his services. He worked outside of the law, but never did anything illegal. Well, most of the time. Stoney didn't like the movie remake with Denzel, it just wasn't right to use the original idea and twist it around. Of course they made it updated and modern, but it just wasn't the original.

She picked up her desk phone and placed a call. She waited until someone answered. "May I talk to Special Agent Maxwell?" She asked and waited until Maxwell came on. "Larry, this is Stoney. I have a new case."

**

Chapter 2

"You know, one day I'm going to make you pay up for all the help I give you," he said.

"I'll tell your wife on you," she said knowing that would stop him.

"That's blackmail and you know it. What do you need this time?"

"Just some background on a woman beater. I should say he's an ex-boyfriend, but he hasn't realized it yet. I'll bring him up to speed."

"What's his name and address, if you have it?"

Stoney asked Marcy to include an address, so she turned over the photo and saw Marcy had written it on the back. Stoney gave the name and address to Larry. He was quiet as he wrote.

"I'll check on this, but give me a little time. They're getting strict about us using the database for personal reasons," he finally said.

"I'm not asking you to look up a girlfriend. I'm working a case that involves domestic violence. It could turn into a case that the FBI would have to investigate. You're just saving me time."

"Okay, I'll run this. I'll call you when I have something," he said.

"Great, say hi to Margaret for me," she said.

"I've never mentioned you to my wife, and I'd like to keep it that way."

"Oh, lover, we were so long ago. You gave me up to marry your wife. Is she the jealous type?"

"You could say that. I don't need to find my manhood missing one night. So let's just leave it at that." He hung up and Stoney laughed.

She put the phone on the desk and sat back, spinning around in the desk chair. She stopped and picked up the photo of the abusive ex and studied it.

Stoney spoke to the photo of Brian. "You are going to regret messing with Marcy. She's my friend now and nobody messes with my friends."

Stoney put the photo back on her desk and thought about her and Larry. It was years ago, she was just starting out as a P.I., before he went into the FBI and after five months their romance ended harshly. Larry had met his future wife and broke it off with Stoney. She hurt badly for a while before getting on with her life, but she never let Larry off that easily.

A woman scorned can be dangerous was her philosophy, but she now depended on Larry for information to help her cases. As an FBI agent he could get better background checks on the men and women she got involved with. Brian was no different.

She stood and decided to go get something to eat. Larry wouldn't get back to her for a while, so she had time to hit her favorite diner. She had gotten used to Coney dogs from when she was a kid running loose on the streets of Detroit. She closed up and drove to National Coney Island, parked and went in.

"Hey, Stoney! The usual?" came a voice behind an opening in the wall to the kitchen. It was Frank, the owner.

"The usual, Frank," she replied with a grin, and went to sit. The waitress brought the food to Stoney and said, "Chasing any bad boys today?"

"I've got one coming up. I just need more information on him."

"Hope you take him down, Stoney," she said and went off to help other customers.

Stoney ate the chili slathered dog and sat thinking about how many of these she'd eaten in all the years. Enough to feed everyone in Detroit, she reckoned. She was surprised that she never got heartburn, but she needed a working heart to do that. She was a person who gave love too easily. Larry was her first real heartthrob, there were a few others, then Doyle came along and she was willing to marry him. No such luck, so she pretty much shut down.

She figured the loss of not knowing who her father was, then the death of her mother, she was left pretty much alone. She didn't socialize with others and had no real friends. Well, there was Avery, the former freelance enforcer who decided that he was going to protect her from the bad elements of the city.

Avery entered her life when she was investigating a murder of a woman. The woman turned out to be Avery's sister. Stoney found the killer and Avery wanted to tear the man apart but Stoney stopped him. Avery wasn't happy, but it kept him from being arrested. Avery said he owed Stoney big time.

She finished the dog and wiped her mouth. It was hard for her to keep the chili from running down the sides of her mouth. She paid the check and went back out to her car, a 2015 Camaro ZL1 that was a gift from a thankful client. He was a car dealer and Stoney had completed a job for him, saving him millions in a divorce. The car was no sweat for the dealer to give her, he had more.

She drove back to her office and went in. The light on her phone was blinking, signifying a message. She hit the recall and listened for the reply.

"Stoney, it's Larry, call me," was all the entire message said. She wondered why he didn't call her on her cell phone, so she called him back.

When he came on he said, "Got some info on your man. Not a nice guy. He has a long history, most recently for assault a number of times from bar fights, and he had a wife, but she went missing. They never found her and he wasn't formally charged for possible murder. Definitely not a nice guy. I emailed you a copy of his rap sheet. If you're protecting a woman from him, tread carefully."

Stoney was too concerned about the news to ask Larry why he didn't call her cell phone. "Nice of you to worry about me, I'll be careful that I don't hurt him too badly. Thanks Larry."

She hung up, turned to her computer and printed out the email, read it and looked at the photo on her desk. "Neanderthal," she said. "I'll send you back to the Stone Age." She stood and closed up the office again. She was going to visit Marcy at her home and see if she knew about Brian's past.

She drove over to the house following the directions she had from Marcy. It was a quiet neighborhood, old houses all spread apart with big lawns. She found the address and pulled into the drive, then went by the garage and looked in the small windows on the doors. She saw a car inside, a late model Ford Fiesta, and the standard items you'd find in a garage. She approached the house and knocked on the door.

Marcy peeked through the curtains and saw Stoney. She opened the door and smiled. "Have you seen him yet?" she asked Stoney.

"No, I just got here. Has he been by yet?"

"No, I haven't seen him. He doesn't go on a schedule, he appears by surprise."

"Well, we have to talk. May I come in?"

"Oh, I'm sorry, yes, please come in." She opened the screen door for Stoney, and stood back. Stoney entered the house. They went to the kitchen table, where Stoney pulled a chair out and sat.

"We need to talk about Brian," Stoney said as Marcy sat.

**

Chapter 3

"Is there something about Brian that I don't already know?" Marcy asked.

"Did you know he has a criminal record? For starters."

She paused and looked confused. "What kind of criminal record?"

Stoney took out the paper with his rap sheet. She spread it out in front of Marcy and said, "You can start back when he was old enough to have a record on file. His sealed record, when he was underage, isn't on here, but I understand he was bad from the beginning. Did you know he was or still is married?"

Marcy's eye grew and she said, "He's married?"

"Well, his wife disappeared two years ago. They never found her, dead or alive, so Brian may be a widower, or still married. Depends on if she's still alive. Brian has five years left before he can declare her legally dead. I don't have any records that he filed for divorce, but I'll look into it."

"I want him out of my life, I don't care if he's married or not," Marcy said firmly.

"I may want to see if I can get him for his wife's murder. Before or after I get him out of your life. If he did murder his wife, I want his hide. You can be assured that he'll be gone from your life, but I'm not done with him."

"You take your work seriously, don't you?"

"Dead serious. I hate injustice and people like Brian who think they can get away with murder. This is not your worry, I just wanted to let you know what kind of man you got involved with."

"Damn, it's so hard nowadays to know who's good or bad. I'll have to run a background check before future relationships with any man," Marcy said without an expression.

"I think it would be a good idea for any woman. Saves on the time spent finding out the man is a bastard. Now I need to catch Brian harassing you."

"He hasn't been around yet today, so it's a good chance he'll be here anytime. If he keeps up the way he's been going."

"How well do you know your neighbor?"

"Jane? She's a good person, why?"

"Can you call and ask her if I can park my car in her drive, just so Brian doesn't see me here?"

"Sure, I'll call now." She stood and placed the call. It was arranged after Marcy explained the situation. Stoney went out and moved her car over. She came back into the house and the two women sat in the living room, waiting.

"How long have you been helping people?" Marcy asked to break the quiet.

"Too long. Too many years and too many people. I don't mind, it's my goal to help. I've succeeded ninety percent of the time, but I've lost a few. I don't think about the failures, they just make me stronger."

Stoney's cell phone rang, she took it out and looked at the caller ID, it said Avery. "Hey bruiser, what's up?"

"I got a call from a fed, he said you may need help," came a booming voice into her ear. Avery was a huge, black monster of a man. He stood over six feet tall and sounded like James Earl Jones.

Stoney figured that Larry had called him. Good old Larry, always worrying about her. "I haven't met the enemy yet, so I don't know if I need help."

"I don't like those odds, girl. Where you at?" he growled.

"Bruiser, I'm fine."

"I know you be fine, girl, but I want to be nearby in case. Talk to me or I'll track you down and you know I can. Save me the trouble."

Stoney paused, then gave him the address. She knew he wasn't going to let it go. Better to have him nearby, than calling her every ten minutes. "Okay, but you hang outside watching. If I can't handle it, then you can come in. But only if I can't handle it, understand?"

"Hey, do I argue with you?"

"Yes, you do," she grumbled back.

"Okay, I'll be nearby, but invisible," he laughed and hung up.

"Who was that?" Marcy asked.

"A friend. He's helped me many times. I owe him a lot." Stoney thought about all the times Avery got involved and even saved her life a number of times. He was her angel. Most of the time she wanted to handle dangerous situations by herself, but Avery always managed to stick his nose in. She just put up with it as long as the case was settled.

They heard a honking outside and Marcy went to the front door. "Don't open the door!" Stoney yelled.

"I was just going to look out the window, to see if it's him," she replied.

"Okay, good. That will let him know you're here. Look out then move away from the door."

Stoney went to the front curtains and peeked out. She saw a GMC suburban parked across the road, honking. She recognized the man at the wheel as Brian and waited to see what he was going to do.

Marcy stood looking out the window in the front door, then moved back. "It's him," she said with a tremor in her voice.

"Come back and sit down. I'll take it from here," Stoney said as the woman sat.

Stoney went to the side door of the house and out. She carefully moved around to the front as she saw Brian Estes get out of the vehicle. She watched him move to the front of the house and up to the porch. Stoney moved around staying carefully hidden by the tall bushes and came up close to the porch.

"Marcy, open the door before I break it down. I've had it with this run around you're giving me. Open up now!" Estes yelled at the door. He tried to open the screen door but Stoney had locked it earlier. That made him mad and he put his elbow into the glass. Stoney figured that was breaking and entering, so she came around the side of the house with her .38 out.

"Estes, freeze," she yelled and moved up to the porch.

Brian looked surprised and said, "You ain't no cop, screw you." He banged on the door and yelled to open up. Stoney shouldered her gun and came up behind him. She gave him one good kidney punch and Estes crumpled.

He recovered and came at Stoney's legs, forcing her to fall back. He came over on her and began punching. She brought her legs up and hooked Estes' body, forcing him off her. She spun around and came up in a crouch. Estes got up and took a swing at her. She moved away and he caught air. She punched him in the side and he yelled in pain.

She stood back and pulled her weapon again, aiming at his head. He froze. "Now sit on the ground or I'll claim you were breaking and entering and I shot you."

He sat and looked up at Stoney. "How the hell is this your business?" he asked.

"Marcy is now a friend of mine and I protect my friends. You are being warned to back off, and leave her alone. Or it may get personal."

"You can't stop me," he spat out.

"No, but I can," came a deep voice from behind Stoney. She didn't need to look back, she knew that voice.

**

Chapter 4

A look of terror came over Estes' face when he saw the huge black man behind Stoney. The man came forward, next to Stoney.

"You did good, girl. I was watching and you took him down in record time," Avery said.

"Are you keeping track of my fights?" she asked.

"Somebody got to," Avery said. "Does you want me to take Mr. Estes here and give him a swim in the Detroit River?"

"No, I'll call Luke Banner and have him taken in for attempted illegal entry and assault."

"Say hi to Luke for me," he said and leaned into Estes. "You're lucky she be turning you over to the police. My idea was much better. Watch yourself, bub. If I hear you harassing Marcy, I'm going to give you swimming lessons. With a concrete block attached to your skinny white ass legs."

Avery stood and grinned at Stoney. "You be good now, ya hear."

"I'm always good, Bruiser. Thanks for the backup," she said as he turned and went off.

Stoney leaned down to Estes and said, "He means it. I'm not going to stop him next time.

Now repeat after me, I will never bother Marcy again."

He looked up at her and repeated the words quietly. "Say it with meaning this time," she said and gave him a kick. He repeated it louder now.

Stoney pulled out her cell phone and called Detective Luke Banner, Detroit Police.

Fifteen minutes later, Luke showed up along with a patrol car following. "Are you still at the protection game, Stoney?"

"You know I am. Caught this creep breaking into this house where a woman lives in fear for her life. Fear of this creep."

Luke looked to the porch were Marcy stood. "Is this the woman?" he asked Stoney. She looked back and said it was. "Did he make threats against this woman, just before he tried to enter?"

"He did. Luckily I was here to stop him from getting to the woman," Stoney said.

"Yes, very lucky," Luke said and told the uniformed officers to take the man into custody.

Stoney took out the rap sheet and handed it to Luke. "Here, to save you some time. I got this from my source in the FBI."

"Larry? I've talked to him about your activities in the past. He worries about you. Was Avery here also?"

"Avery? Avery who?" Stoney said with a grin.

"That's a yes on his presence, I presume. I have nothing against Avery, as long as he doesn't murder anyone deliberately."

"He only shoots when necessary, same as I do," she said demurely.

"So what's the story on this guy?"

"He's been abusing the woman, she wanted him out of her life and I had a talk with him after he tried to get at her."

"You're just a regular Wonder Woman," Luke said with a smile. "You know he'll be out by tomorrow. B&E isn't a big deal crime."

"Maybe I should have let him hurt the woman, would you be able to keep him for a few more days? Domestic violence cases are touchy. Short of murdering her, he skates easily enough. Maybe I should have let Avery take him swimming."

"I didn't hear that. But privately, it would have saved me a lot of hassle. Well, I have to go book him and file a report. Later, beautiful." He turned and left.

Marcy was still on the porch as Stoney came up to her. "He's been warned, but he'll be out by tomorrow after posting a small bail. I'll have you watched until I'm sure he's taken the hint."

"Do you think he'll be back?" Marcy asked nervously.

"I'll be honest, I don't know him well enough to say if he took the hint to stay away. He was warned, so next time it will be harder on him. Not by the police," Stoney said.

"Thank you, Miss Hawk."

"I would think you could call me Stoney by now," Stoney said with a smile.

"Thank you, Stoney. What do I do now?"

"Get on with your life. What do you do for a living?"

"I'm a court reporter," she replied.

Stoney thought about that, "Did Brian know that?"

"Sure, he was in court when we met. He wasn't a criminal, just there as a witness. He started to talk to me in the lunch room and we hit it off. I should have known better than hooking up with someone from the court room."

"Not a great place, but better than a bar, I guess. What was he witness to?"

"For the defense. A friend of his was being charged with assault and Brian spoke about how his friend was the victim."

"Seems Brian has a lot to do with assault. I'll have someone watching you for the next couple days, just to see if Brian shows back up. Don't worry, you won't see my friend watching, but he'll be there."

"Will it be that big black man I saw threatening Brian?"

"Yes, and it will be the last time you see him, unless Brian shows back up. So, again, don't worry. I have to go in and file a complaint against Brian, to help keep him in jail. I'll call with any information you need to know." Stoney turned and went across the lawn to the neighbor's drive to get her car.

A woman came out of the house and over to Stoney. "Excuse me, I was watching the police take that horrible man away. Is he gone for good?"

Stoney smiled and said, "I hope so, or he'll regret it. Do you know the man?"

"Just from seeing him bothering Marcy. I almost called the police a few times but he left before I went to call. I could tell he was trouble by the way he acted."

"If you could keep an eye out for him, I'd appreciate it if you would call me," Stoney said handing her a business card. "Thanks."

Stoney drove back to her office and found Avery sitting in his Chevy SUV. Big man, big car. Stoney parked and went to her office door followed by Avery. They went in and Stoney checked her answering machine, and found nothing.

"Is your bad boy in custody?" Avery asked.

"Luke had him taken in. I'm going into the precinct to press charges and talk to Luke about the creep's missing wife. Just to see what I can find out."

"You're not letting him off the hook that easily, are you?" Avery grinned.

"Nope, if he did his wife in, I want to be the one to find out. Can you keep an eye on Marcy for me, just until you're sure Estes is going to heed your warning?"

"I got my thermos of coffee and my favorite CDs in the car all ready to camp out on her street. You can be assured she will be all right. You think he may come back?"

"He must have figured that Marcy brought me in to scare him off, so he may not like it. I think he may take another run at her. Let's be real careful, he's got a record of violence and the missing wife, whom he may have killed."

Avery grinned. "He's the one who needs be more careful with me around."
**

Chapter 5

"Just don't hurt him too badly. I want his hide for when I prove he murdered his wife," Stoney said.

"Think he did it?"

"Well, it stands to reason, by his actions towards Marcy. He's an abuser and probably always has been."

"I could just beat the truth out of him, if he did murder his wife," Avery grinned.

"Thanks, but I'll get the facts that will convict him without torture. But it's a good thought, as a last resort," Stoney said with a sly smile.

"Do what you got to do, girl. I have to go find a camping spot to protect your client," Avery said with a wide grin, and left the office.

Stoney closed up her office and drove to the precinct where Estes was being held.

She went in and straight to Luke's office. She had been there many times in the past, mostly to be questioned as to why she shot someone. She found Luke sitting at his desk going over some papers.

"It never ends, does it," she said standing at his door.

"What? The paperwork? Hell no, and people like you make more work for me."

Stoney entered and sat at his desk, in the chair she knew well. "If it weren't for me, your job would be a lot harder."

"You're in a position to be hired to work a possible crime. We don't know what's happening until it's been committed. By then it's too late for most victims. Yes, I appreciate that you stop a crime or worse, murder, it makes things easier for me. But according to the law, what you do is sketchy. I have to word my reports carefully to get people like

Estes convicted and not set loose by some high priced lawyer, because a woman with a private license stopped a crime in progress."

"Thank you, too," Stoney said with a smile. "Now I need to know all you have on Estes. He must have files in the system about his wife who disappeared two years ago."

Luke sat back in his chair and swiveled back and forth. He sighed and said, "I don't think you listen to me most of the time."

"I listen to you, lover. I just have my own set of priorities." She reached to a small jar on Luke's desk that had jelly beans in it. She liberated a handful and sat back popping one into her mouth at a time.

Luke sat staring at Stoney, "Why do you want to know about this guy's missing wife?"

"Just a feeling that he may have murdered her. Do you have anything on him?"

"I haven't gotten into his file yet. You gave me most of the information from Larry that I would want."

"That was just his rap sheet, I want to see his file about the case against him."

"Did this take place in Detroit?" Luke asked.

"I should have asked more from Larry. He probably has most of the case files in the FBI system. I'll call him if you don't have anything."

Luke turned to his computer and punched a bunch of keys. He waited then said, "He has a file but as you said, the FBI took the case and I don't have anything on him. You know how the FBI hates to share their cases with us local cops."

"I'll go track down Larry and get that from him. Thanks, Luke. Is Estes going to post bail?"

"In the morning, I'm sure. We can only hold him so long until he has to see the judge and that could be next week. We're busy with crime in Detroit, if you haven't heard," Luke said with a fake frown.

"Yeah, yeah. I'll talk to you later," Stoney said standing.

"I'll need your statement about the break in and the assault on you," Luke said as Stoney was leaving.

"I'll get it to you," she replied and went out.

Back at her car she stood looking around the area. It was in a nicer section of the city, away from the slums and the less desirable people who would end up in jail for what they would do to survive. The poor and the drug users would rob people and homes daily to live. Stoney wasn't a bleeding heart for the lesser creatures that inhabited the city. She preferred they all go away, but since they wouldn't, she had to do her job to stop them.

She drove out and over to the new FBI building down by the city hall. She parked and went in to the front desk and asked for

Larry Maxwell. The agent at the desk asked her to wait as he made a call. He finished the call and asked Stoney to wait.

Stoney walked around the lobby being checked out by the men coming and going. Her attire was bordering on hooker and she didn't care.

Larry came out of a hallway and to her. "You just had to visit me?"

"Larry, lover, I need some information and you have the juice to get it."

"Fine, and don't call me lover in the building. It doesn't go well with my image." He turned and went back to the hallway, followed by Stoney.

"Where are you taking me, lover?" she said loud enough to be heard by the agents nearby. Many a head turned to them.

Larry spun and pointed at her. "Look, I cooperate only because we have a past. I don't need my job or my name to be made a laughing-stock. Please respect that."

"Sorry, Agent Maxwell. I'll keep my distance." She smiled at him.

He turned back, muttered something obscene, and went to his office and in. "What do you want, that brings you here to my world?"

"I want all the info you have on Brian Estes. Especially about his missing wife. I presume you haven't found her?"

"As I understand, it's still an open case. Hang on," he said and went to his computer. "I suppose you want a copy of the reports?"

"That would help," Stoney replied.

"You know I don't have to give you this. It's an FBI file and you aren't FBI."

"You could just leave it on your desk and I could steal it."

"Don't say steal around here. You could borrow it, without my knowledge. That still may not work but I can say I didn't know you took it. I have too many years in the agency to lose my job."

"I'll protect your integrity and job. Does Estes have a jacket in your system?"

"He does, but it's not available right now. If you can be patient, I'll see if I can liberate it and slip it to you. But not right now, I'll get it to you tomorrow."

"Okay, I can wait. His wife has been gone for two years, so she can wait one more day," Stoney said and went to leave. "Oh, and we really should get together for lunch sometime. You and the wife, me and Avery. Now that would be something to talk about." She laughed out loud and went out the door.

Larry sat back and wondered what god he insulted to have Stoney in his life.

**

Chapter 6

Stoney drove away from the federal building and was deep in thought. Not about Estes, but about her office move out of the city. She had most of her cases here in Detroit, would there be as many in the suburbs? She'd probably die from following cheating spouses out there. The city was where the most action and crimes happened, so maybe she should hang in a little longer. Besides, it would be a pain to move all her office equipment to a new place.

She pulled into the office parking area and sat studying the building. It had character and was old. It looked like whoever had an office there had experience and it was crucial for her clients to believe she could handle the job. The office building she looked at in Sterling Heights was a modern building, lots of glass and chrome. It now felt like a harsh environment for her to be working out of. She hadn't signed any agreements yet, so she could cancel the move.

She went to open her door when she saw a note stuck in the crack of the door. She pulled it out and unlocked the door, going in. She sat at her desk and opened the note. It was handwritten and was a warning.

"Stay away from Brian Estes, or you'll regret it."

She set the note on her desk and tried to keep from laughing. It just seemed to be a juvenile attempt to intimidate her into staying away. She knew it would never happen, and wondered who would have put the note in the door. Estes was in jail, so it had to be an accomplice. One of his buddies who he talked to after his arrest. The note just gave her cause to want to get more into the murder of Estes' wife.

She wondered if this note was because she stopped Estes from bothering Marcy, or the fact that she wanted to open the missing wife case. No one but Avery, Luke and Larry knew about her interest in the wife. She had mentioned to Marcy about his wife being missing, but didn't say she was going to investigate it. Besides, why would Marcy say anything to Estes' friends, if she knew any?

She knew she had a rough ride ahead with Estes. Men like him don't give up easily. She had seen a show on TV about a true case where a woman is beaten unconscious and left in a garbage bin by her abusive ex-husband on the fifth anniversary of their divorce. Five stinking years after they were divorced. These men just don't forgive and forget. Stoney wished there was a way to legally murder all the abusive people.

She turned when she heard her door open. A man came over to her desk and stood smiling. "Larry said you were good-looking, but I think he underestimated you."

"Larry? As in Maxwell?"

"The one and the same. He asked me to deliver a package to you and to help you with the situation you are interested in. I'm Special Agent Russ Holt, and I was the agent in charge of the case of Brian Estes' missing wife. Maybe we can help each other. I really got to disliking Estes, he was an arrogant bastard and I'd like to see him go down. We get so backed up in our bureau, that I was told to put the case on the back burner then."

"I would love to have some help. I'm not one to deny it when I want to see justice done. What do you have? Please sit down," she said and motioned to the chair next to her desk. Holt sat and put a folder on her desk.

"Do you know anything about Estes?" he asked.

"All I know is he was abusing my client, and she wanted him out of her life. Larry mentioned about the missing wife when he gave me Estes' rap sheet."

"Then you at least know he's a rotten one. To set up the events, two years ago this month, we were called about a missing woman. The caller identified herself as a friend of the victim. I'm calling her a victim, but I don't know if she was murdered or if she just ran away from Estes. We went to talk to the friend and she filled us in on Estes and his abuse of the wife. The friend also said that she wasn't sure if Lisa, that was the wife's name, had run away or if Estes did her in. She had been missing for a week, before the friend got concerned and called us."

"Was this friend a neighbor?" Stoney asked.

"She was. We finally went to talk to Estes, and asked if his wife was present. He got nasty and said for us to get off his property. I warned him that I could get a warrant to search his house or he could let us talk to his wife. He said she was out of town visiting relatives. I questioned him as to where these relatives lived and he got nasty again claiming he didn't know them that well."

"He didn't know where his in-laws lived? That sounds suspicious. "

"That did send up flags for us. He wouldn't let us in the house and said we'd have to talk to him through his lawyer. He slammed the door and we left. We couldn't get a warrant; the judge said we didn't have enough evidence as to whether the wife was missing or just visiting relatives. We talked to the neighbor again and she didn't know where any relatives could be. I got a new case assigned to me that took more of my attention, so I held on to this until now. We did assume it was just a wife running away from an abusive husband. We find this becoming more prevalent all the time. Especially with the many new domestic violence shelters springing up."

"Maybe I can check with the local DV shelters and see if she used one," Stoney said.

"They don't like giving out names or information about clients. Maybe I could go along and show my badge. It may help," he said with a grin.

"I'm sure a big, strong, good-looking man with a federal badge could woo the info out of them. Especially with a smile like you have," she said with a great smile of her own.

"Stoney, are you flirting with me?"

"Don't get all flustered. I love to mess with people's heads and you aren't above that. I'd welcome you going with me. Shall we make a field trip of it?"

"I'd be glad to. When?"

"It's getting late now, so how about early tomorrow morning?"

"I'll be here when you open. I'll drive."

"What? You don't trust a woman to drive?"

"It's not that, but Larry warned me about you and said to never get in a car with you behind the wheel."

"Really? I'll have to have a talk with Larry. I don't need him playing father figure. I'll see you in the morning."

Russ grinned, gave her his business card and left the building. Stoney sat back and watched him through the window going to his car. This should be interesting, she thought

**

Chapter 7

Stoney called Avery and explained about the note on her door. "Be on the alert for anyone approaching Marcy's house. Estes may be still in jail, but it looks like he has friends."

"I'm ready for anyone, girl. They best be tougher than I am, or they'll go down," Avery growled into the phone.

"Just leave a little of them so we can find out what the deal is. I can understand Estes' problem with Marcy, but why would he involve friends?"

"The man is a psycho, what do you expect?"

Stoney told him about Agent Holt's visit. "It may be good to have a fed with me when I go deal with the bureaucracy at the DV shelters."

"Feds always good to have along, if you aren't a criminal," he laughed. "Is he good-looking?"

"Avery, you know better than to ask that," she said.

"I'm just wondering if he be your next conquest."

"I don't conquer every man I meet," she replied.

"Only good looking law enforcement types."

She thought on that. All her love interests were with cops, so it could be true. "Okay, I have pinned a few badges to my bed post, but that doesn't make me a sucker for cops."

"No comment, girl. I'll call if anything develops here," he said and hung up.

She spun around in her chair again, thinking about Agent Holt. He was good-looking and had a nice physique in his Brooks Brothers suit that she could see. She had an image of him naked in the sunlight, with her lounging before him.

She shook her head and had to get her mind back on Estes. It was getting late and she was wired now. She stood and closed up the office, turning back to have one more look. She decided to stay here, the suburbs were too tame.

She decided to go to her favorite watering hole, Vinnie's Lounge. She enjoyed the place and its ambience of early mob rule. Vinnie had long since been dead, from a hit by an unknown assailant, so the place had a history. She grew up nearby, not far from the lounge and had her first drink there when she could pass for being old enough. They never questioned her age, she was too good looking to turn away. Mike, the forever bartender, had served her that drink and he still served her every time she was there. He had to be in his eighties but still looked healthy and wise.

Stoney entered the building and over to her favorite seat at the bar. Mike came over with her usual drink, a Miller, and placed it in front of her. "What's happening, Stoney? Shoot anyone today?" Mike asked,

"Not yet, Mike. The evening is still young," she replied.

He gave a hoarse laugh, too many years of smoking, put his elbows on the bar, and leaned to her. "You know Stoney, you need to settle down, get married and have kids."

"I hope you're being funny, Mike. It's the furthest thing from my mind. You know my lifestyle; I don't slow down for much."

"I hope you don't end up in an early grave. We get too soon old and too late smart," he said in his best Yiddish, laughed again and coughed hard. "I need a smoke," he said and went off.

Stoney shook her head, out of sympathy for the man. He had been a fixture in the bar since before Vinnie was murdered in the fifties. Stoney had not been born yet to have known Vinnie, but she heard all the stories about him and his life. It would make a great movie, she often thought.

She sat waiting for the door to open and in would walk the two men who she saw follow her from her office. The men in the car behind her weren't very good at tailing. She spotted them right after she pulled out of her parking lot.

She waved to Mike and pointed to her drink. He nodded and brought her another. "Mike, do you still have your scatter gun behind the bar?"

"Never leaves my sight. Why, you got trouble coming?"

"Could be, two men followed me here and I'm waiting for them to come in."

"Don't you worry, I'll be ready in case," he said and looked under the bar to be sure his sawed off shotgun was there.

The bar wasn't busy for the time of day. Most people were home having dinner or getting off work. She looked around at the ten or so people sitting at various tables, talking. She heard the front door open and watched in the mirror behind the bar at the two men coming in. Mike was busy washing glasses but was keeping an eye on the men.

They walked past Stoney and sat at the bar about five stools away. Mike asked them what they were drinking and they asked for beer on tap. Mike filled two mugs and placed them in front of the men.

"I ain't seen you two around here before. New in this area?" Mike asked them. They just sat staring at him and saying nothing. "Sorry to bother you," Mike muttered and walked down towards Stoney. "Nice friendly guys," he said to her.

Stoney got up and went behind the men. She turned and put her hands on each man's shoulder, saying, "Why don't you tell me why you've been following me?"

The men put their hands into their jackets just as Mike pulled the scatter gun and slammed it on the bar. "Answer the lady's question and slowly take your hands out from your coats." Mike growled.

The men eyed the shotgun and sat up straight as Stoney stepped back a little, prepared for anything. She reached under her leather waist coat and pulled the Berretta from its shoulder holster. She held it at her side, so not to upset the other people in the bar.

She went to the side of the man on the right and leaned on the bar, bringing up the Berretta to his side. "What are you to Brian Estes? One of his buddies, or a partner in crime?"

The man looked over to the other man and they stood. Stoney stood back waiting for trouble. They turned away, saying nothing and left the bar.

"How rude!" Stoney exclaimed. "I should have shot him." She went back to her beer and sat. She suddenly stood back up and went to the front window and looked out to her car. The two men had gotten in their car and then driven out.

"I had this thought that they might damage my car, but they didn't," she said sitting back on the stool.

She pulled out her cell phone as Mike put his gun back in its holder under the bar. "Hey, Bruiser. I just had two gorillas follow me to Vinnies. They left the bar without even saying a word. I guess they didn't like my company. Be on the lookout for a grey late model Crown Vic cruising the neighborhood."

"They already went by about an hour ago. I snapped a few photos of the car, I'll shoot you the images later. They didn't try anything?"

"Nope, and with Mike's persuader they couldn't do much damage," she said.

Avery laughed and said, "Mike be a man after my own heart."

**

Chapter 8

"Okay, we have more trouble coming if Estes has his buddies working with him. I'll call Luke in the morning and see where Estes stands on the charges. I may want to tip his hand by not pressing charges and let him off. That will free him up to do something more stupid."

"Works for me," Avery said. "So far all is quiet here, unless Estes' boys come back. I'll call you if I see them again."

"Thanks, talk to you later," Stoney said and hung up. She signaled to Mike for another beer and sat wondering what was so important to Estes that he involves others in his love gone wrong. Was there more to the story than she could see?

She finished the beer and flipped a ten on the bar, waving to Mike, and left. At her car she looked around and didn't see anyone watching her. She drove out and went to her apartment.

She lived spartanly, very little furniture and no decorations on the walls. It reminded her of when she was young and poor. Even if she was making good money on the big cases that she worked, she saved her money frugally. She tossed her keys on the kitchen table and went to the refrigerator taking out another Miller. She realized that she would have to exercise a little harder this week to work off what she downed tonight.

She sat on the easy chair next to the small couch and put her feet up on the footrest. The remote was on the arm and she clicked around the channels but found nothing to watch. She turned it off and heard a noise coming from the bedroom.

"Loki!" she yelled. "What are you doing?"

She watched the bedroom door open slowly and smiled as the ferret stuck its nose around the door. The bouncy creature came flying out and over to her, jumping up on her lap. He snuggled up to her as she stroked his fur. "How's my evil little god of pranks doing tonight? Did you miss me?"

The animal looked up to her and tried to chew on her thumb. She thought back to when she first found the animal on a case. It was in a cage, malnourished and looking half dead. She brought the ferret home and nursed it back to health. She didn't worry about letting it run loose, since there wasn't anything in the apartment that Loki could get in trouble with. She had a large cage in the bedroom for the animal to poop in a box and rest in the little hammock at the top.

Her phone rang, startling the ferret and she took it out of her pocket. The ID said Avery. "What's up?" she asked.

"I got visitors, interested in coming over?" Avery said.

"What are they doing?"

"Just sitting in their car watching the house. I'm ready to move on them if they even get close to the place. I thought maybe you might want to question them."

"Give me a couple minutes and I'll be there. Leave some skin for me if you have to take them on." She hung up, stood and put the animal on the couch. She went to get a warmer jacket and petted the ferret before leaving. She drove out and over to Marcy's house trying not to break any speed limits, but in a hurry.

She figured where Avery would be parked and pulled up behind him with her lights out. She looked around and could see the Crown Vic parked down the street with the men just sitting. Stoney got out and went around Avery's car and slid into his passenger seat.

"Nice night to spy," Avery said with a wide grin, showing plenty of teeth.

"How long have they been here?"

"About forty minutes, just sitting. Five minutes before you came, I saw one answer a phone. Maybe Estes checking in?"

"Could be, but a person in jail can only make collect calls. Can't do that on a cell phone."

They sat and watched the men still sitting and watching. About ten minutes later they opened their doors and got out.

"Post time," Avery said with a smile.

"Let's just wait to see what they do first," Stoney replied.

The two men walked up to the house and stood just off the porch. One man went to a window and tried to look in.

"We got us a peeping tom," Avery said. "Shall we bust him?"

"Not yet, when they go for the door, we'll attack."

The two men went around the side of the house towards the back.

"That's not good, we need to move now," Avery growled.

"Agreed," Stoney exhaled and opened her door. They got out and ran to the house. "Go around that way," Stoney said and pointed to the other side of the house. Avery went that way as Stoney followed the men. She stopped and peeked around the corner of the house, she didn't see the men. "Damn," she mumbled and rushed to the back.

She stopped by some tall bushes on the corner of the house and looked between the building and a tree. She saw the men standing in the backyard watching the house. The moon was out tonight providing a little light to see them by. She wondered what they were going to do now.

She was sure Avery had them in his sights and wouldn't do anything until Stoney moved first. She watched them talking quietly to each other and then one man moved towards the house. She moved out a little to see what he was up to. The man went to a window and looked in. He signaled to the other man and waved him to come closer. They both stood at the window as Stoney moved quietly behind them. Avery moved to her side.

"You know it's illegal to peep on a woman," she said softly.

Both the men turned quickly and looked shocked. Stoney and Avery already had their guns aimed at the men.

"This time I want you to talk to me, guys." She pointed to the one man closer and said, "Start talking."

The back porch flood lights suddenly went on, temporarily blinding Stoney and Avery. That gave the men a chance to run. Stoney fired in their direction, but they were around the corner already. She didn't want her bullets to go astray and hit an innocent person so she stopped. Avery was already moving in their direction as Stoney looked up to the door and saw Marcy looking out.

"Get back in and close the door. Bolt it, too," Stoney yelled as she moved off towards the front. She saw that the car they came in was still sitting there, empty. They must have run out in to the neighborhood and hid. She didn't see Avery, but she was sure he was hot on their tracks.

She went down to the street and stood listening. She didn't hear anything, which worried her. She heard someone running around a house next to Marcy's and pointed her gun in that direction. It was Avery. He came out from the side of the house and over to her.

"Again, they didn't say much, did they?" he said with a frown.

**

Chapter 9

"Well, we have their car. They'll have to hoof it now. I'll call Luke and see if he's still on duty," Stoney said and pulled out her cellphone.

"Were you waiting until I was just about to get off my shift before annoying me, Stoney?" Luke replied.

"Sorry, but crime knows no schedule. I have a car for you to impound." She gave the Reader's Digest version of her night from Vinnie's bar to chasing the two men in the neighborhood.

"Avery couldn't stop them?" Luke said.

"Circumstances. They always get in the way," Stoney said with a laugh.

"I'll be right over. Try not to shoot anyone," he said and hung up.

Stoney turned to Avery, "Luke is on his way," she said and walked to the Crown Vic. She opened the driver's door and looked in. The car was clean, no mess. She figured they'd have empty beer cans on the floor and a full ashtray. But she saw nothing like that.

"I wonder if this is a stolen vehicle?" she said to Avery as he came up behind her.

"The good old boys didn't exactly party in the car, did they?" he said.

"With the vehicle VIN number and plates, Luke should find out who the car belongs to. I'm sure if it comes down to it, fingerprints will give them away." She closed the door and opened the back door. She leaned in and brought out a shotgun. "Well, it's not hunting season. Why would they have this?"

"Two legged prey," Avery said with a grin.

Stoney put the shotgun on the top of the car and looked in again. "This backseat looks like they just cleaned it, but I can see what looks like blood in the cracks of the seat. I'm sure forensics can find out if it's human."

She stood out of the car and looked around the neighborhood. "If they did something illegal, I would think they'd want this car back. Keep your eyes open."

Avery already had his back to the car and was scoping out the area. "Let them come, I be ready."

"I would think you'd be a great target from the side of a house. Maybe we should move to the other side of the car until Luke and his troops get here."

They moved around the car and stood watching. Nothing was moving in the barely moonlit night. Shortly, three patrol cars and one unmarked car drove up with flashers, no sirens. Luke pulled close to the Crown Vic and parked.

"Which way did they go?" he asked Stoney. She pointed to Avery and he pointed towards a row of houses.

"That be the way they went," he said smoothly.

Luke called to three of the officers and told them to canvas the area for the two men. They ran off and disappeared around the houses. Luke came up to Stoney, "You are full of excitement tonight aren't you?"

"Just protecting my client. These men followed me around earlier and then came here to sit and watch Marcy's house. They went into the backyard and we followed. Unfortunately they didn't say anything before they made a break."

"Okay, I have forensics coming to check the car then we'll haul it in." He saw the shotgun on the roof of the car. "Yours?"

"Not my style," Stoney grinned. "It was on the backseat floor. Looks like there are traces of blood on the seat, but your team will determine that."

"Could it be Estes' long lost wife?" Luke asked.

"After two years? I doubt it. Unless she was alive up to when they finally murdered her."

"Where would they keep her alive for two years?" Luke asked.

"Maybe you should look into Estes' house and see. As a matter of fact, I'd like to see in his house."

"He hasn't committed any crime that would allow us to search his home. You could only look into it illegally. But that's never stopped you," Luke said with a laugh. "Just don't get caught." He turned when the CSU van pulled up and parked.

"Now we'll get some answers," Stoney said. She and Avery moved away from the car as the team came over to talk to Luke.

"You feel like a midnight raid on Estes' domicile?" Avery asked Stoney.

"I think it's on the agenda, care to join me?"

"I like going through people's houses. Just to see how the other half lives."

"I still have his address, shall we take our leave of this mess?"

"Only if lover boy can part with you," he grinned.

"Stop that, I never was intimate with Luke. I think he may be gay, but don't quote me on that. It's just my feeling," she said.

"Right. Any man who would turn you down must be gay."

"I didn't say he turned me down, he just never tried. Now drop my love life and let's go." Stoney went to Luke and said she was leaving.

"Stoney, I need your statement," he replied.

"I'll drop it off in the morning. It's getting late and I need my sleep."

"Don't nap in Estes' house," he said quietly.

"I'm a light sleeper." She turned and went to Avery. They went to their cars when Stoney stopped. She turned to Avery and said, "Those two bozos are still at large. I don't think Marcy should be left alone with them still out there."

"Gotcha," Avery smiled and went to his car and got in. Stoney went to her car and drove out. She remembered the address of Estes' house and knew the street. She drove until she found the street. It wasn't very well lit, no street lights along the road. She took out her handheld spotlight and shined it on the houses until she found the address. She parked in front and got out.

The moon had gone behind clouds so she wasn't going to be seen very easily as she went up to the house. She went around the back and to the door. She had her little tool kit in her back pocket and took out the instruments to pick the lock.

She was surprised to find the door was not locked. She took out her gun and carefully pushed open the door. It was dark in the house and she brought her mag flashlight from the car. She entered a kitchen and stood listening for noises. She didn't figure Estes would do anything illegal in the house, except in the basement. She found a door off the kitchen and opened it. There were stairs going down so she carefully stepped down into the darkness. She found a switch on the wall and flicked it. The basement lit up brightly, so she shut off her flashlight.

She reached the bottom and looked around the room. She could see the basement windows were covered with cardboard, which she thought was interesting. Estes didn't want people seeing what was in the basement. This was good for her, since the lack of lights wouldn't attract attention from the neighbors.

There were a number of boxes piled up in the room, and a freezer on one wall. She felt a chill thinking what could be in the freezer. She went to it and lifted the door.

**

Chapter 10

The freezer cover was heavy but she held it up as she looked into the icy depth. There were large parcels wrapped in white paper reminding her of the slabs of meat her mother would buy from the butcher. She propped up the door and reached into the freezer, pulling up one wrapped parcel. She took it to a small table and started to unwrap it.

Inside the paper was a rack of ribs. It reminded her of ribs from a cow that she had seen before in her youth. It wasn't from a human, much to her dismay. She opened two more packages and found the same, animal meat. She rewrapped the packages and put them back in the freezer. She opened a few boxes scattered around the room and found nothing of interest. Mostly hoarded items from the life of Brian Estes.

She closed everything back up and checked the basement walls for any hidden rooms. She found nothing.

"Well, this was disappointing," she said to the air.

"You be disappointed? That's not good," came a voice from the stairs. Stoney whipped out her gun and spun to the intruder. It was Avery.

"What are you doing here? What about Marcy?" she demanded.

"Marcy be all right. Estes still in jail and your playmate Luke caught the two men hiding in a garage next to Marcy's house. He has them in custody. Marcy be safe for now."

"So you decided to come here and protect me?" she said holstering her weapon.

"I thought it would be a nice gesture," he said with a wide grin.

"Well, there's nothing down here. I need to check the upstairs, if you'd care to help, it would save time."

"Anything to get you out of this house," he said and turned back up the stairs.

Stoney followed him thinking that this could be a futile attempt. Estes had to be smarter than to leave the dead body of his wife in his house. A search warrant could end his deceit real quick. Or a snoopy P.I. who doesn't worry about breaking and entering.

Stoney and Avery did a quick search of the house and found nothing of interest. Stoney did find that all female clothing had been removed from the house. Evidently Estes didn't plan on his wife coming back.

"I got nothing, babe," Avery said, coming out of the bathroom. "The place is clean, like the car. Estes being careful or just a neat freak."

"I'm not satisfied that he's innocent. The man is an abuser and if his wife got under his last nerve, she's buried somewhere. It's too dark out to look for a grave. After two years it would be impossible to find it, anyway. Let's go visit Luke and see what he is going to do with the men."

They headed out the back door and Stoney made sure it was locked. Avery said he would follow her, and went to his car. Stoney started her car and drove to the precinct where her two mute men were locked up.

They went in the station, through the squad room and found Luke at the door to the interrogation room. He turned to them and gave a surprised look.

"I didn't figure the both of you would be here, but it's fine with me," Luke said, eyeing Avery.

"I'm no criminal, detective," Avery said, with a wide grin. "I be a peace-loving citizen who helps a crazy woman P.I. in her endeavors to fight crime."

Luke laughed and said, "I was just going in to question this guy. The other is in the next room."

"You want Avery and me to question him?" Stoney said looking as serious as she could.

"No, I'd like him alive when I talk to him. Go in the middle room and watch through the mirror." Luke left them and went into the room. Stoney and Avery went into the observation room and watched Luke sit across from the man, handcuffed to the table.

The man was sitting quietly, not showing any emotion or agitation for being shackled. He didn't look at Luke, just stared at the table.

"According to your driver's license your name is Bailey Crump. Interesting name. Why were you at the home of Marcy Esper?"

The man just sat and stared at Luke, not saying a word or showing life in his eyes. Stoney looked at Avery and said, "What is it with these guys, don't they have tongues?"

"Look, it would be better for you if you'd talk to me," Luke said to the silent man. "If you don't, I'm going to talk to your buddy, Kenny. Maybe he'll give me something to go on and I'm sure he'll walk faster than you do."

The man showed no interest. Then he said, "You can do what you will. I'm not talking without my lawyer."

Luke looked to the mirror and gave a frown. He stood and said, "Fine, sit here until we find your lawyer." He turned away and left the room. He went to the other interrogation room as Stoney and Avery turned to look through the other mirror in the room. Luke entered the room and stood staring at the man, also shackled to the table.

"Now what kind of lies are you going to tell me, Kenny? Your buddy, Bailey, was a real chatterbox, but I don't believe him. So, Marcy Esper was on Brian Estes' hit list and you were going to murder her."

Kenny's eyes lit up and he sat up straight. "What are you talking about? We weren't going to murder anyone. Bailey is crazy to say that. Estes wanted us to threaten the woman, and that was all."

"Threaten? For what?" Luke asked.

"To shut her up about the abuse he gave her."

Luke looked at the mirror and smiled. He turned back to Kenny, "Was Estes abusing the woman?"

Kenny went silent.

"Did he abuse her like he abused his wife?" Luke asked.

That got a reaction from Kenny. "Hey, I had nothing to do with his marriage to that bitch. What he did to scare her away was his business. He never told us what actually happened to her. He did say she ran away."

"That I can believe. He abused her to the breaking point and she left him, right?"

"I guess so. He never said," Kenny said quietly.

"But he did tell you he was abusing Marcy Esper?" Luke said and waited. Kenny didn't respond. "Well, think, Kenny. Why would he tell you to threaten her into denying she was abused?"

Kenny looked confused. He was now acting uncomfortable.

"Why are you protecting him? He's a waste of life for abusing a woman. Are you in favor of abusing a woman, Kenny?"

That got a reaction. "Hell no, I respect women."

"But you went to Marcy's house to threaten her. You call that respect?"

"I wasn't going to do anything. Bailey likes that shit. He beats his wife all the time. He knows how to hit women and not leave bruises. I was just going along to back him up. That's all."

Luke turned to the mirror again and frowned. Stoney said to Avery, "I'd like a few minutes alone with Bailey."

"I'm sure you would, babe." Avery said with a grin.

**

Chapter 11

"Why were you following Stoney Hawk?" Luke asked the man.

"Who?" he replied.

"The tall, good-looking blonde woman," Luke told him.

"Now Luke thinks you're good-looking," Avery said to Stoney in the observation room.

"Knock it off, Avery," Stoney replied. "I want to hear this."

Luke asked the man again, "Why were you following her?"

"Brian told us to. If she went to see Marcy, we were to warn her to stay away."

"Warn her? Now that would have been interesting to see. How would you have accomplished that, by beating her up?"

"Whatever it took to convince her to lay off Marcy."

"So your job was to warn Marcy not to talk about being abused and warn Stoney to stay away, using whatever method to scare them. Right?" Luke asked. He pushed a pad and pen to Kenny and told him to write all that down and sign it. Kenny was busy writing as Luke smiled at the glass.

"That's about it," Kenny said as he finished. "Is this what Bailey told you? He probably blamed me for it all,"

"Actually, Bailey wanted his lawyer, so he told us nothing. But you were cooperative, so I may see to getting you a lighter sentence. Thanks, Kenny." Luke turned to the door and went out as Kenny was protesting.

Luke went into observation and smiled. "Well, we can get Heckle and Jeckle for attempted threats and possible assault on witnesses, then get Brian for conspiracy to intimidate and threaten. I don't know if the charges will stick, but we can hold them for a while longer. But you know they'll get out on bail."

"We'll be waiting at the front door when they get out," Stoney said with an evil grin.

"Don't go doing something stupid. I don't want to have to arrest you," Luke said, smiled and went out the door. Stoney and Avery followed as Luke told a couple officers in the hall to book the men on conspiracy to commit bodily harm, trespass, and coercion. The officers went to take the men to central booking.

"Now what?" Stoney asked.

"Up to the judge. If they get good lawyers, they'll skate. They both never touched you or

Marcy so that is a point in their favor. All we can do is hope."

"What about Estes?" Avery asked.

"Well, we have Kenny's testimony that Brian Estes hired them to intimidate and threaten witnesses, so he may get a harder slap on the hand. Time will tell."

"It's late and the unholy three will be held until tomorrow, if they can post bail. I'm ready for some sleep," Stoney said. She looked at Avery and said, "Shall we go?"

They said their goodnights to Luke and left the building. At the cars, Avery said, "I'll check with you in the morning to see where we stand with Estes and his crew."

"Good, I'll talk to you then," she replied and got into her car. She drove back to her apartment and went in. Loki was up on the couch sleeping and jumped up when Stoney came in. He ran to her and she lifted him. "You're getting fat, I need to get you on a diet," she told the ferret and gave him a kiss.

"You also need a bath," she added, wrinkling her nose.

She was too tired to hit the shower with the ferret so she went into the bedroom and put the animal on the bed. He stood up for her as she undressed and then spun around and plopped down on the comforter. She smiled and crawled under the covers, thinking about her trip in the morning with Special Agent Holt. She'd have to call Luke first to see what the status was on Estes, then call Avery.

She lay there for a short while then fell asleep.

She felt a bouncy object on her head and squinted open one eye to see Loki on her pillow, pulling on her hair. She grabbed him and put him further away. She looked at the clock and it showed seven-fifteen. She forced herself up and went into the shower followed by the ferret. She slept in the nude so she just walked into the shower stall, followed by Loki. She turned on the water and soaped up, then reached down and rubbed some soap on the ferret at her feet. He shook off the soap and danced around the rain of water, getting good and wet.

Stoney finished and stepped out, reaching for a towel. She dried herself, then the ferret. He went streaking out of the room when she opened the door. She stood at the bathroom door, wrapped in a towel, when she heard a noise at her front door. She went to get her gun and came back to the living room when she heard the noise again. She peeked out the peep hole and saw Luke standing there on his phone.

Stoney's apartment phone started ringing and she figured Luke was calling her. She opened the door and he jumped. "If you're calling me, you can hang up," she said. "Come in."

Luke was eyeing the towel, "I didn't interrupt anything, did I?"

"Just got out of the shower, but as a detective, you must have figured that out."

"Yeeow!" Luke yelled when he saw the ferret coming at him. "You got a big rat in your apartment!" he yelled.

"Geez, haven't you ever seen a ferret before?" Stoney lifted the creature and held him up to Luke.

"No, thank you. I grew up with lots of rats in my neighborhood, I don't like them. Hell, some were as big as cats."

"Well, Loki is not a rat, and he's very gentle." She put him down and he bounded off down the hallway.

"Loki?" Luke said.

"The god of pranks. He fits the name. I have to keep an eye on him when I leave my keys on the coffee table. He'll grab them and hide them. Ferrets like to hide things. Now what are you doing here so early?"

"I was in the neighborhood and thought I'd drop by and let you know that Estes and his men are going to stay locked up for a few days more. The DA gave a stirring testimony and they were given a high bail. Which they couldn't afford right now."

"You could have called to tell me this?" she said giving him a squinty eye.

He laughed and said, "I'd like to take you to breakfast."

"I'd love that, but I have a date."

"With who?" Luke asked.

"Special Agent Russ Holt. We're going to track down Estes' missing wife."

"You're getting help from a Fed?"

"Sure, Larry had him come to see me with the case files from the original disappearance of Estes' wife. Holt was lead agent on that investigation."

"Ah, Larry. Your old boytoy. How is old Larry?"

"He's good and he's happily married now. Jealous?"

"Me? Never."

"Well, you had your chance but blew it. I often wondered if you were gay, turning me down like you did."

"I had my reasons. You weren't the girl for me, sorry."

She smiled, dropped her towel and said, "See what you missed." She laughed and went into the bedroom.

**

Chapter 12

Luke's mouth dropped and then he closed it quickly and cleared his throat. He could hear Stoney laughing from the bedroom.

"I'll just leave you to your date. I'll call later, when I know more about Estes," Luke yelled towards the bedroom. He turned and left the apartment, before Stoney could stop him.

She came out to find he was gone. "His loss," she said to Loki, looking up at her, and went to get ready to go out with Agent Holt.

She gave the ferret his food, then left for her office. On the way over she tried to figure out Luke. She didn't think he was really gay, but he never took her advances and went with them. Maybe he had a girlfriend he wasn't admitting to. Now she was really curious and decided she was going to find out his dark secret. Mostly to ease her mind as to why she couldn't entice him.

She arrived at her office and found Agent Holt standing by his car. It was an FBI issued black Crown Victoria and it was old. Holt must have been out of favor with his office to get such a crappy looking car. She parked and got out.

"Are you being punished?" she asked as she passed by him.

"What are you talking about?" he asked.

She turned and pointed to the car. "Does that thing go over forty miles per hour?" she laughed.

"Hey, I've used this car for many a chase and it holds its own," he replied as he followed her to the door. She unlocked it and entered. Holt followed.

"So, are you ready to go shake some trees as to where Lisa Estes disappeared?" she said and went to check her answering machine. There was one message from Marcy asking about Estes and if he was getting out today. Stoney had no answer for her yet.

"I compiled a list of the DV shelters in the Detroit area, there are only two that have been around since Lisa Estes vanished. There are two more but they are more recent ones, so she couldn't have gone there."

"We'll go check the two that might have her on record, but I have to place a call first." Stoney picked up her desk phone and called Marcy. She wondered why Marcy hadn't called her on her cell phone, but she did say that was for emergencies only. The phone rang a couple times then Marcy answered.

"Marcy, it's Stoney. Just wanted to tell you there's been nothing new about Brian. He may have to sit in jail a few more days, unless he can come up with the bail money."

"I just wanted to know what to expect," Marcy said.

"I'll be sure to call you when I hear something. Just go about your daily routine and wait for my call."

They said their goodbyes, then hung up. "Okay, we can go now." Stoney headed for the door and Holt followed her out. She locked the door as Holt was heading to his car.

"Oh, no. I'm not riding in that death trap. We'll take my car, it's newer and in better shape," she said going to her car.

Holt was going to protest but he was warned by Larry that she was bull-headed. He went to her car and got in. "You better drive safely," he warned.

"Buckle up," she replied with a grin and started the car. She sat a moment then pealed out of the parking lot, causing a high-pitched sound from Holt.

"Easy, we're in no rush," he said nervously. "She's been gone for two years, one more afternoon isn't going to be a problem."

"I just wanted to see how your nerves were. Wuss," she said low.

"I'm not a wuss. I just don't like not being in control of a vehicle," he retorted.

"Plus, Larry warned you about me," she said bringing the car under control out into traffic.

"Yeah, that," he said. "Let's get safely to the DV shelters, can we?"

"Fine. Where's the first one?"

He gave her the address and she drove carefully through the traffic to the building. It was old and needed fixing up, but it served the purpose. Stoney parked in front and they went in.

They went to a reception counter and stood as a rather large black woman came to them. She looked at Holt, then Stoney and said, "Dropping her off?"

Stoney laughed and said, "Hardly. If anything he would need shelter."

The woman eyeballed Holt as he took out his badge and said, "Special Agent Russ Holt,

Detroit FBI. We need to talk to someone who took care of clients about two years ago."

"You don't want much, do you? Hold on, I'll call the supervisor. She's been here a couple years." The woman turned and went to a phone on a desk. She was talking to someone and then hung up. She looked back and said, "Mrs. Walker will be with you shortly."

They stood waiting in the small lobby when a door opened and out walked another black woman, a little older and dressed nicely in a beige suit. "I understand you're with the FBI? May I see your credentials?"

Holt took out his badge wallet and turned it to the ID card, handing it to the woman. She studied it then handed it back.

"I'm sorry, but we get men coming in here pretending to be law enforcement looking for a woman in the shelter. We have to be careful with our clients. Now may I help you?" she said and looked at Stoney.

Stoney Hawk

"I'm Stoney Hawk, private investigator and Agent Holt and I are trying to find a woman who we think was possibly murdered two years ago. Agent Holt thought she may have run away from her husband and came to one of the shelters in the city."

"You want me to dig back two years and see if she came through here?"

"It would really help. It would help us to close the case and possibly convict the husband for murder," Stoney said.

"Well, we don't usually give out sensitive information, but if it would help, I'll see if she came through here. Now remember, a lot of women don't use the shelters, they sometimes go to relatives out of state."

"I thought of that but we don't know who her relatives were," Holt said.

"And I suppose the husband isn't cooperating on that?"

"Hardly, he's in jail now for abusing a girlfriend. But he'll be out in a few days, which is why we want to find out about the wife so we can put him away for good," Stoney said.

"Well, in that case, I'll see if I can dig out the files from back then. Follow me, please." She led them through a door and in to a large room with many file cabinets and desks. There were a number of workers busy on paperwork and ignoring them.

"What date was the disappearance reported?"

Holt opened the file he was carrying and gave her the range of dates that she was reported missing. The supervisor went down the row of cabinets and stopped at one. She opened the cabinet and asked for the name. Holt told her.

She thumbed through the file folders and pulled one. "Here it is."

**

Chapter 13

Stoney's heart sank ever so slightly when she thought the woman did come here and wasn't murdered. Not that she wanted the woman to be dead, but it would help Stoney to take down Estes if she was.

The supervisor took the file to a desk and sat. She motioned to Holt and Stoney to sit also. They did.

"Okay, Lisa Estes was admitted to the shelter on the last date you gave me. She stayed here for three days then released herself saying she was going to visit a cousin in Ohio. I have the address if you'd like it?"

Holt said they would and the woman wrote it down. "I don't know if the phone number will still work, but you can try."

"Thank you, Mrs. Walker," Stoney said. "You've saved us a lot of tracking. Is there anything in the file about her husband?"

"We did take photos of bruises and a black eye he gave her. She refused police assistance and we have to respect the client's wishes. There's not much more about the husband. Our social worker talked to her and reported she was despondent about the last incident with her husband. She just wanted to be away from the man."

"Thank you again," Stoney said. "I think we can find out if the woman is still alive through the cousin. It's a big help."

They all stood and the supervisor took them back to the main entrance. They said their goodbyes and left.

In the car Stoney took out her cell phone and dialed the number on the paper the woman gave them. She listened for a moment when someone answered. Stoney put the phone on speaker and said, "Ma'am, I'm a private investigator in Detroit and were trying to locate Lisa Estes. Do you know her?"

The woman hesitated then asked, "Who are you?"

"My name is Stoney Hawk and I'm with Special Agent Russ Holt of the Detroit FBI. We talked to a domestic violence shelter here in Detroit and they gave us your number. We are trying to find Lisa. It was reported by the DV shelter that she moved from Michigan to Ohio two years ago. Is Lisa still living with you?"

"Lisa contacted me two years ago and said she was coming to live with me for a while until she could get her life together. I knew what her miserable husband was like and told her to come. She did and stayed here for two months then said she had a job back in the Detroit area, and moved back there. She never called to say what she was doing. I gave up waiting for her to call, I didn't know how to reach her."

"Do you remember what company she was going to work for?" Stoney asked.

"She only said it was a temp agency, something like Troy Temps. That's all I remember, sorry."

"That's a big help to us, thank you." Stoney said goodbye and hung up.

"There is a Troy Temps in the city of Troy. I had to investigate a kidnapping and murder of one of their employees. Feel like taking a ride?"

"Lead the way," Stoney said with a smile.

"Go to I-75 North and get off on Crooks Road. I'll explain from there."

Stoney hit the gas as Holt held on to his seat belt tightly. He was dreading her getting on the freeway.

Thirty-five minutes later, they came to Crooks Road and Holt showed her the rest of the way. He relaxed now that she was on city streets with lots of traffic. They arrived at Troy Temps and parked.

"I'm surprised it's still here," Holt said and got out of the car.

They went in and the office was quiet, only two women at their desks. One woman looked over to them and stood. "May I help you?" she said going to them.

Stoney let Holt take lead since he was involved with this company already. Holt took out his badge and showed it to the woman. "Special Agent Holt, Detroit FBI. We need some information on a woman who came here two years ago for work."

"Two years? That's a long time. What was her name?" she asked.

"Lisa Estes," Stoney offered.

The woman stood thinking. Then she turned and went to her computer and did some typing on the keyboard. She watched as the computer brought up a file and she studied it for a moment.

"Yes, she worked for us for about two months then she went out on a job and didn't come back. The only reference I can find about that last job was a call from a man named Bailey Crump, strange name, and he said he needed this woman named Lisa Estes. He knew her from another job she worked and said they wanted to hire her full time. I gave Lisa the info and she left. We didn't hear back from her."

"Bailey was too stupid to use a fake name," Stoney said to Holt and asked the woman what the name of the company was.

"Argo Computers, on Cadiuex over by Harper," she replied.

"Thanks," Holt said and they left. He stood by Stoney's car and said, "This is becoming a scavenger hunt. Follow the clues to all points until we get a solid lead. If Bailey did draw her to the business, then Estes had to be behind it."

"Took him a while to track her down. I doubt Argo Computers would know Lisa." Stoney took out her cellphone and got on Google, looking up the computer store's number. She called and got in the car. Holt sat listening to the phone ring, then it was answered.

"Argo Computers, how may I help you?"

"I need to talk to a supervisor. One who's been there a long time," Stoney asked.

The man said "Just a moment." Then he put them on hold as they listened to crappy hold music. They waited.

"We could have driven there faster," Holt said, just as someone answered.

"May I help you?" the voice asked.

"I'm looking for one of your employees, his name is Bailey Crump. Is he still employed with you?"

"No, we canned his butt a year ago for being a lousy employee. Who are you?"

"I'm a private investigator and I'm looking for a missing woman who we understand was going to work for your company. Her name was Lisa Estes. Do you know her?"

"No, but I knew another Estes, his name was Brian. He worked here also and was also fired for being a jerk. Sorry, I don't know this Lisa you're looking for."

"Thank you for your time," Stoney said and hung up. "Well, it seems that Brian was trying to draw Lisa out from hiding. And he evidently succeeded. We need to talk to Luke Banner and have a chat with him about his prisoners."

They drove back to Luke's precinct and went in. They found Luke in his office and he was surprised to see them.

"Hey, Russ, how are you doing? Did you get stuck with Stoney today?"

"Yep, covering a cold case that involves a couple of your prisoners. Stoney filled me in on the mess they did, and we have new information about the missing wife of Brian Estes."

"Well, have a seat and fill me in."

Everyone sat and talked about what Stoney and Holt found out on the missing wife.

"You've been busy. Now we have something to badger Crump into admitting. I'll get him and Estes in interrogation and we can do a little con on them." Luke picked up his office phone and placed a call to have the men taken to separate rooms. "Shall we go see if we can beat a confession out of someone?"

**

Chapter 14

"Do you think you can get a warrant to search Bailey's house?" Stoney asked Luke.

"I can get one faster," Holt said. I'll call my SAIC and get it set up. Do you have his address?" he asked Luke.

Luke opened a file and gave him the address from the man's driver's license. Holt called his office and made arrangements to send agents to the address after getting a warrant. He then called in for the warrant explaining the circumstances and was assured it would be done.

"Okay, those wheels are turning. Hopefully there will be some evidence in Bailey's house. I don't think Estes would be dumb enough to leave any trace around his place," Holt said.

"I didn't see anything when I went through it, but I never said that," she said with a grin.

"Okay, shall we go have a talk with Bailey first?" Luke said.

They left the office and went to the room with Bailey sitting impatiently. Luke, Stoney and Holt came in and pulled chairs to the table. Bailey was eyeing them and looking concerned. Especially when he saw Stoney.

"What's this? Are you all going to take turns beating on me?" he asked.

"Well, you're talking now, how nice. We just have a few loose ends to tie up before we prosecute you for murder," Luke said leaning forward.

"Murder? I didn't do any murder," he said nervously.

"You already know Stoney Hawk. The gentleman to her right is Special Agent Holt, FBI. He and Stoney have been following a trail that leads back to you, Bailey. A very convoluted trail. It seems that Lisa Estes, your buddy Brian's wife, ran away from him and ended up working at a temp agency in

Troy," Luke paused for effect. "We don't know how you found her there but we have it on record that you called and requested her to work at Argo Computers. But she never showed up for work. Not a good way to start a new job. But then you wouldn't know about a good job since Argo fired your sorry ass, along with Brian Estes. We have to assume you led Lisa to the company and then you and Brian abducted her. What did you do with the body?"

Bailey was looking completely panicked now. "I don't have the body. Brian got rid of her after we brought her to my house. I told him I didn't want her there and he killed her and took her out to Belle Isle and dumped her there. Or so he said."

Luke looked at his friends and said, "I'll see if a body was found out there. That will give us our corpus delicti if it proves to be Lisa." Luke looked back to Bailey, "We have enough evidence that you coerced Lisa Estes into being taken and murdered. Whether you did it or not. But if you can finger Brian for the actual murder, maybe I can see if you get a lighter sentence."

"Hell, man, I'll sign any confession that he killed her. He strangled her with his bare hands. I'm sure if they have the body it will show that's the way she died."

Luke pushed a pad and pen to him and said to write everything that happened back then, including when Estes put him up to calling the temp agency to send Lisa to Argo. Bailey started writing fast and furiously.

After he finished, Luke stood along with Stoney and Holt. They left the room and went down to see Estes in his room. They stood outside looking at him in the room through the window, acting cool and comfortable.

"No sign of worry or regret. He's a worthless piece of crap," Stoney said. "Can I interrogate him, alone?"

"No, Stoney, you can't. I don't see any reason to even talk to him. We got most of what we needed from Crump. I'll call and find out if a body was found on Belle Isle, and if it can be identified now. Once the body is identified, I'll place him under arrest for murder. I'll even let you give him his rights, Stoney. Think you still remember them?"

"I do, thanks," Stoney replied.

"Thanks for the leg work, guys. I was hating the thought we may have had to turn him loose. I'll go check on the body. Be back shortly, it's mostly paperwork, since we can't dig her up now."

He went off as Stoney said, "Well, that was simple. All in one day. Now you can brag to your fellow agents that you cleared the cold case in record time."

"With your help. Shall we get a cup of coffee while we wait for Luke to get back?"

"I don't drink coffee, but they have soda pop in the machine. I could use a Pepsi."

They headed to the break room and sat. About an hour later, Luke found them and sat at the table.

"It's a go. The body was strangled by hands according to the autopsy. The description I had from the original case matched the body. If we can get some finger prints from the house, they will have a definite lock on the body."

"I called and they got a warrant and are searching the house now," Holt said. "If forensics gets some prints we'll shoot them to you."

"Thanks. I'm always happy when a case closes. We'll have to celebrate," Luke said.

"I have to call Marcy and let her know. This should end her problem." Stoney stood and went out in the hallway and pulled out her cell phone. She hit the speed dial and waited. After a couple rings Marcy answered.

"Marcy, it's Stoney. Good news, Brian won't be bothering you for a long time. We're going to file for murder charges on his wife."

"Oh my God, he was a murderer and I was involved with him. Could I have been murdered also?"

"It's possible, but he's been stopped so forget him and any time you spent with him. Get on with your life and be careful with men you meet. Call me and I'll investigate them for you," Stoney laughed as did Marcy.

"Are you sure I can't pay you for what you did?" Marcy asked.

"No, but you can send a hundred dollars to the women's shelter in Detroit. That would be payment enough."

"I'll send it in your name, Stoney. Thanks, will I ever see you again?"

"Only if you're in trouble again, call me." They said their goodbyes and hung up.

Stoney Hawk

Stoney stood in the hallway thinking about the last couple days. She'd have to call Avery and let him know it was over. She speed dialed Avery and he came on right after the first ring.

"Whatcha got, babe?" his booming voice came through the phone.

"Good news, Estes is going down for murder. We got him with the evidence and a body."

"A body after two years. That must be ripe," he laughed.

"No, bruiser. Luke went by the autopsy from the body. We're ninety percent sure it's her."

"That's close enough. So I don't get to watch Marcy now?"

"You aren't at her house right now are you?" Stoney asked.

He was laughing and then said, "No comment."
**

Chapter 15

"Okay, I have nothing better to do. I'll give her one more night of security, then I'm out of here," Avery said.

"You're a good person, Avery. Thanks. Talk to you tomorrow." Stoney smiled and hung up.

Stoney went back to the men still seated at the table. She sat and asked, "Are we going to arrest Estes?"

"I just called the DA and gave him the info. He said we're good to go for an arrest. Shall we go give the good news to Estes?" Luke stood and they all went back to the interrogation rooms. They came up to the room where Estes was and looked in.

Estes was gone.

"Ralph! Where the hell is Estes?" Luke yelled to a guard.

The man came up and looked in. "Shit! He was in there." He opened the door and went to the table, grabbing the cuffs still attached to the table. They were still fastened but the cuff holding Estes was opened.

"Lock down the precinct," Luke yelled to the guard as he ran out. "Damn, how did he get loose?"

Stoney said, "You know these cuffs aren't foolproof. If he had a hairpin or paperclip, he could have worked his way loose while we sat in the break room."

"Fine, let's split up and go find him." Luke ran out of the room as Holt and Stoney followed. Stoney stopped in the hallway and told Holt she had to make a call.

He said he'd talk later and ran off. Stoney speed dialed Avery and waited. He came on and said, "Do you miss me already?"

"Avery, Estes escaped from the precinct, keep an extra eye out. He may want revenge on Marcy for some odd reason."

"Don't you worry, babe. I got this situation. You go find him." She said she would and hung up.

She stood there annoyed this was happening. So near to closing the case and frying Estes, but now he was out there somewhere. She couldn't think of where he would go. His friends were locked up and she didn't know anyone else he knew. But he could go to Marcy and think he could hide out there. Taking Marcy as a hostage. She went out as there was chaos in the squad room. Everyone was rushing around looking in all the places Estes could hide. She saw Luke and went to him.

"I'm going to head out to a place he might go if he got out of the station. Tell Russ if you see him where I went."

"Where are you going?" Luke asked.

"To Marcy's house," she said and ran out the door passing through the barricade of cops watching for Estes.

She made it to her car and jumped in. She sped out and watched for Estes along the way on foot, but didn't see him. Her cell phone rang and she answered. It was Luke.

"Stoney, Estes managed to take a patrol car. He's off into the streets. I got an APB and a BOLO out for him. I don't know if he is hitting the back streets but be careful."

"No, he better be careful of me, if I get him," Stoney uttered roughly.

"Stoney, be careful, don't kill him," Luke said.

Stoney hung up as she got to Marcy's street. She didn't see a patrol car parked on the street, she looked for Avery, but didn't see him. She cursed that he may have left. She pulled up to the front of the house and jumped out, running to the front door. She pounded on it but got no answer.

She ran around the back and pounded on the door, but got no answer again. She knew Marcy had been home, since she talked to her earlier on the phone. She looked around for Avery, figuring he would come out now that she was there, he didn't.

She moved to the alley behind the house and was stunned to see a patrol car parked behind the garage. She ran back to the house and ran at the door with her shoulder. It exploded open and she rushed in.

"Estes, if you are in here, I'm coming for you!" she screamed. It was silent in the house, then she heard a noise. It was a muffled sound, like someone protesting their mouth being gagged. She ran into the living room and turned to see Estes with his arm around Marcy.

"Let her go, Estes. You won't get away from me," she yelled at the man holding her gun out.

"Screw you, bitch," he said as he moved Marcy towards the door. He had a knife at her throat.

"You know you just screwed your chances at just one murder. Now you got kidnapping and attempted murder. That's a death penalty."

"Michigan has no death penalty, bitch," Estes yelled back at her.

"I'm not talking about the justice system. I'm talking about that big black man who told you he'd take you out if you came back."

"Yeah, but he's not here, I saw him leave," he replied.

"You didn't look behind you, Estes."

Estes turned towards the big picture window and left his body open to Avery standing outside the window aiming his .357 at Estes. The man looked like a deer caught in headlights at the sight of the man, as Avery fired at him.

Estes spun around releasing Marcy and fell to the floor. Stoney ran to him and grabbed the knife Estes had. She felt his neck and couldn't find a pulse. Oh well, she thought

She stood as Avery entered the house. "He's gone. Good riddance." She pulled her cell phone out and called Luke, explaining that Estes was dead.

"Did you have to shoot him?" Luke asked.

"I didn't, Avery did and he saved Marcy. So he's a hero and should be given that much. Estes was going to kill Marcy and Avery stopped him."

"I'll be there shortly," Luke said and hung up.

An hour later, the cops, M.E. and forensics were combing the house. Luke had Marcy off the side talking to her. Avery was out on the front lawn with Holt. They were laughing and talking. Stoney stood on the porch looking at the sky. The stars were barely seen through all the light from the city. What she could see were beautiful.

Luke came up behind her and said, "Marcy backed up your story. I have no problem with Avery shooting Estes. It solved a lot of problems. So Marcy is safe now."

"What about Bailey Crump?"

"He'll do some time for his part in the murder of the wife. Not much can be done for him."

"Kenny?" Stoney asked.

"He was just stupid and followed his buddies. I doubt he'll get much time. What are you going to do now?"

"I may take some time off and relax," she said.

Luke smiled and gave her a kiss on the cheek. "That can be construed as sexual harassment," Stoney told him.

"So lock me up," he said back. "Now, excuse me, I have a date."

"A date? Male or female?" Stoney asked.

"Stoney! I told you I'm straight. My date is with a fourteen year old girl, my daughter, if you must know."

**

Chapter 16

Stoney was struck by the answer. "You have a daughter? I didn't know you were married."

"I'm not. Well, I was. My wife died a number of years ago in a drive-by shooting aimed at me. I blamed myself for her death. My daughter was too young to understand the implications. It was hard and it took a lot of my free time to give her the attention she needed."

Stoney now realized why Luke had cast off her attentions. "I'm sorry. It must be hard to deal with her at that age. I know I was a real hellion back then at the same age. Can I talk to her and give her some advice on growing up?"

"Are you kidding? I don't want her growing up to be like you. You're dangerous," he laughed. "But you've been through tough times. It may help, just be easy. I'll arrange for a time that we can get together. Just give me some time."

He went off. Stoney watched him walk away, with a new respect for him. A single dad, a cop, trying to raise a daughter in Detroit. A train wreck waiting to happen. She hoped she could help.

Avery came up with Holt and they stood by her as she turned to them. "What are you two plotting?" she asked

"Nothing, babe. Are you good?" Avery asked.

"I'm fine, I got some answers to a burning question and a case closed. We need to celebrate. How about a pizza at Cloverleaf?"

"Sounds good," Holt said.

"I'll meet you there," Avery said and walked away.

"He's not coming. He hates pizza," Stoney said to Holt. "It will be just you and me."

"I love pizza, especially Cloverleaf. What shall we do after that?"

"Are you afraid of ferrets?" she asked with an evil grin.

**

THE END

~~*~~

Here's a free chapter preview of the next Jim Richards book, "Lonely Hearts Murders"

Chapter 1

I was surprised to see my daughter, Carol, standing at my office door. I was also surprised that Lacey hadn't made a big deal out of her being in the building. My office manager would never pass up a detail like Carol being here, without warning me.

"What are you doing here? You're always so busy at Angelo's cooking up a storm." I asked.

"I know, but I have a problem and I hoped you could help," she said, moving into my room. She looked worried and then sat in my client chair.

"Okay, I'm here for you, tell me what's up?" I turned my attentions to her and waited. She now looked distressed. I continued to wait, giving her the time to let it out.

She finally said, "I have a friend who may be in trouble."

"What kind of trouble?" I asked when she stopped talking.

"That's just it, I don't know. She's missing." She went silent again, wringing her hands and looking at the floor.

"Carol, have you talked to the police?"

"I don't have anything to give them. No evidence that she's actually missing, or how long she's been gone."

"Okay, start at the beginning. Who is your friend and why do you believe she's missing?"

"Her name is Sue Hanson, I've known her for about a month. She was a new employee at Angelo's, working as a waitress. We got along well and she was a very nice person.

She didn't come into work two days ago and since then has been missing. She has no family here in Las Vegas, so there was no one to report her missing."

"I presume she had no friends?"

"Just me and two of the other girls at the restaurant. I talked to them and they don't know where she is. I know she's new in town, but to just disappear like that, so soon after starting a job, it's not right."

"Tell me about her. Whatever you know, or she told you."

"Well, she came from a town in Missouri and moved here about three months ago. She saw an ad Angelo put in the Review-Journal for a waitress job. She told Angelo that she had experience and he hired her. She was a happy person most of the time, but she told me she was lonely without having someone, a man, to share with. She said she had a boyfriend back home but they broke up. So she moved here for the excitement and glamor."

"Boy, was she wrong," I said. My tiny toy Yorkie, Willy, came rushing in the room and over to Carol. She reached down and picked him up.

"Hey, baby, how are you doing?" she asked as Willy was trying to lick her hands. Carol laughed and looked back to me. "Do you think you could see if she's all right?"

"Well, I don't have much to do lately, so I could give it a quick look. Do you know her address?" I asked.

She dug into her purse and pulled out a card. She handed it to me. "She gave me this after we started to get to know each other a little better. I hope you can find out what happened to her."

"I'll do my best, but she may have decided that she didn't like Vegas and went back home. Or found a different job."

"I don't think she would do either of those things without talking to me. We had a nice bond together."

"We all have things that we don't share with others, so don't feel bad if she didn't confide everything in you," I said.

"I know, I guess it was nice to have a friend to talk to. I've been so busy at the restaurant, I haven't had much time to get to know anyone. Besides, in Vegas there are not many places to find a friend. Although Sue did mention a place called Lonely Hearts. It's a match type company for people looking for dates."

"Those places are just as bad as meeting people in a bar. They never look into a person very carefully, just a few questions and a photograph, then they set a person up with whomever has the money to look through the photos of other lonely people."

"You sound like you've been there," Carol said with a grin.

"Okay, in my youth, I tried a couple of the dating places. I also paid a small fortune for nothing. I did better in a bar."

"Did what better in a bar?" came a voice from my door. It was Penny. She always popped up when I said something incriminating. Just so she could interrogate me. She breezed into the room and over to Carol. "Carol, it's so good to see you outside of the restaurant. Have a day off finally?"

"I'm starting to cut back on my hours. Angelo is not happy, but he understands I can't die in the kitchen."

"Are you just visiting or have a crime for Jim to solve?" Penny asked, sitting next to Carol. She reached over to take Willy, who was squirming.

"I have a small problem, maybe. I thought maybe Dad could help."

"What is it?" Penny asked.

"A missing friend," I answered her. "I'm going to check out the friend and see if she's all right."

"Good, I have nothing better to do today, I'll go with you," Penny said with a smile.

I cringed at the thought, but it couldn't hurt to take her. She could come up with good ideas that often helped to solve cases. Not that I hoped this would become a case. I hoped the missing woman just was doing something better than being a waitress. "Fine, you can come with me."

"Good that you made up your mind. When do we go?"

"Be patient. Carol, what are you going to do today?"

"I have to go into work, since Sue left we're a little short of help. I'll call you later and see if you found out anything." She stood and said her goodbyes.

We watched her leave and Penny turned to me. "Where's Lacey? I came through the lobby and she wasn't there."

"I don't know. I haven't been out of my office this morning. She wasn't out there?"

"No, I stood and waited, but she's missing."

"Great, more missing persons. Is this an epidemic?" I said and stood. I went out followed by Penny and Willy, heading for the front lobby

The desk where Lacey held court was empty. Something that was odd. She hardly ever left the desk for very long. I called her name loudly and listened. Then I heard a small voice coming from the doorway to the side offices, where Lynn, Deacon and Buck were located. Along with the break room and lounge.

"I'm busy," was the reply from behind the door. That sounded like Lacey's demanding voice.

"Are you all right?" I yelled back. The door opened and she came out followed by a bouquet of helium balloons, one of which said 'Happy Birthday.' She tied them to her chair.

"Now, do you need me?" she asked.

"Uh, whose birthday is it?" I asked.

"Jessie, I found out when she was born and it's today."

**

Continued in the book…

More books by Bob Moats

The Fatal Series - Fatal Rejection * Fatal Departure * Fatal Romance * Fatal Outbreak * Fatal Abduction * Fatal Seance

Doyle, P.I. Series - Doyle's Law * Doyle's Justice * Doyle's Quest * Doyle's Paradise * Doyle's Haunting

Bob Moats

NEW for 2015 - The Gus Mackie novella series - Gus Mackie and the Hot Tamale * Gus Mackie and the Missing Princess * Gus Mackie and the Weeping Wife * Gus Mackie and the Lost Heiress * Gus Mackie and the Rock Star

Also Bob's first juvenile book, "Crystal Prison of Kyr"

The Jim Richards books by Bob Moats

(In series order)
Classmate Murders
Vegas Showgirl Murders
Dominatrix Murders
Mistress Murders
Bridezilla Murders
Magic Murders
Strip Club Murders
Made-for-TV Murders
Mystery Cruise Murders
Talk Show Murders

Stoney Hawk

Sin City Murders
Black Widow Murders
Vegas Vigilante Murders
Area 51 Murders
Mortuary Murders
Hypnotic Murders
Sunshine State Murders
Blue Suede Murders
Honky Tonk Murders
Dark Carnival Murders
Lipstick Murders
Pasta Murders
Talent Show Murders
Shyster Murders
Campground Murders
Network Murders
Reunion Murders
Big Apple Murders
Kennel Murders
Trick or Treat Murders
Santa Murders
Wiseguy Murders
Toxic Murders

For a preview or to purchase a book, go to
http://murdernovels.com

Bob Moats

Jim Richards Family of Readers

Thanks to the following people who are now part of the Jim Richards Family of Readers. They have read a book or more and enjoyed them. They all volunteered to be included in the list. If you are a fan of the books, send me your full name and you will be included in future books. Send your name to murdernovels@bobmoats.com to be added in the books and on the website.

* Achim Feifel * Al Norris * Alex Wheatley * Alexandra Delporte-Wilkinson * Amy Morningstar * Andrea Bryan * Anne Shepherd * Arianda Sugar * Arlene Markowski * Ashley Augustus * Audra Hall * Barbara Hughes * Barbara Sammons * Barbara Schuler * Barbara Zirger * Beth Donohue Plenskofski * Beth Rosin * Betsy Childress * Beth Gibson * Betty Albrecht Vollmar * Bill Sandy * Bill Tornquist * Billie-jo Collie * Bob Lenski * Boni J Rychener * Candace Larson * Carl Bishopric * Carla Lewis * Carole Henderson * Carolyn

Conroy * Carolyn Riddle-Linington * Casey Moats * Cassy Bailey * Cathie Turner * Chad Hudson * Charlie Meier * Charlotte L Duran * Cheryl L. Everett * Cindy Ackley Nunn * Cindy Valstad * Connie Bancroft * Corinne Kay O'Daniel * Chris Krolczyk * Dana Robbins Chuchran * Dana Wichita * Daniel Kalus * Danielle Monique * Darren Heald * Dave Travers * David Wilkinson * David Wiman * DeAnn Jannereth * Deanna Miller * Deb Breuker Balbo * Debbie Carter * Debbie White * Deborah Fartuch * Deborah Gauze * Deborah Sullivan * Dee King * Denise Freeman * Devdatta Arun Gholkar * Diana Carver * Dianna Marie Juneau * Dianne Procopio * Dixie Beck * Donna Gould * Donna Thompson * Donny Minter * Doris Kight * Eddie Moore * Eric Walters * Felicia Annette Bradfield * Fleur Wilkinson * Francine Menor * Gail Chesney * Georgiann Minster * George Conner * Greg Colucci * Hayley Rankin * Harold Garcia * Heidi Arnold * Herb Muir * Irma Ranee Coy * Jack Plunkitt * Jacqueline Moss * Jan Kimball * Jane Lawson * Janice Schneider * Janice Spoor * Jeanette Mulroy * Jennifer Besner * Jennifer Redmond * Jerry Dornak * Jessica

Bob Moats

Keown-Belous * Jim Beck * Jo Boguslaw * Joela Quaine * Jo Turner * Joanne Marie Turner * Joanna Wisniewski * John Gross * John Peiffer * John Wisbiski * Joseph Wauro * Joyce Stacy * Joyce Trifiletti * Judy Franklin * Judy Travers * Judy Padgett * Julie Heath * Junnahvee Benson * Justin Moats * Karen Dahl * Karen Grams * Karen Higham * Karen Kaiser * Karen Meinburg Richwine * Karen Kirkman Parker * Karin Hawkins * Karin Vasvari * Karn Jones * Kathleen Donohue Roesing * Kathleen Riddle-Wolfe * Kathy Hinds Moore * Kathy Jones * Kathy Mitchell * Katie Benzler * Kay Burns * Kelly Garcia * Ken Boggs * Keota Rodriguez * Kiera Mccarthy * Kim Estes * Kimberley May * Kitty Stolle * Kristie Sciler * Kirsty Stanton * LaLonnie Scallen * Larry Morris * Leann Parr * Lenora Scales * Leslie Marie Jackson * Linda Forester * Linda Bartley Florence * Linda Ingle Cox * Linda Kennerö * Linda Magill * Lisa Bower * Lisa Keller * Liz Gibson * Lorraine Wiman * Loretta Alexander * Lynda Bowles * Lynette Lawrance * LuAnn Louttit * Manny Rothman * Marcia-Lee Finocchio * Marcia Gibson DeWitt * Marie Calder * Marlene Bryan *

Stoney Hawk

MaryLouise Kramp * Mary Lynn Gross * Megan Atkins * Meghan Hyden * Melissa Wescoat * Melody Cannavan * Meredith Simko Hanak * Michael Carruthers * Michael Dinkens * Michael Vannoy * Michelle Burns-Mitchell * Michelle Pilcher * Micki Potter * Mike Moats * Mikki Gregory * Mimi Baur * Merri Taylor * Myrna Hecht * Nadine Sutton * Nancy Ellen Sayre * Nancy Graveman Davis * Natalie Quine * Neena Martin * O'Della Wilson * Pamela Cooke Malone-O'brien * Pat Pollington * Pat Rohn * Patricia Jarmon * Patricia C Trezza * Patrick Barry * Paul Lawrance * Peggy Davis * Phyllis Bassett * Ray Zink * Raylene Matheny * Rebecca Collins Besner * Renee Brumley * Reta Hanna * Reta Moats * Robert Lenski * Roberta Meister * Roberta Navarro-Harder * Sally Berneathy * Sally Hubler * Sandy Sillman * Sandy Schuman * Sara Swope * Sarah Santos * Satka Nikc * Sharon E. Edwards * Sharon Mangini * Sharon McMillon * Sheena Rawl * Sherry Amstutz * Sherry Tull * Shirley Alvarez * Shirley Davies * Shirley Williams * Stacie Rowe * Stephanie Conner * Steve Cullen * Sue Payne * Susan Haughton * Susan Hesse Adams *

Susan Salomon * Suzan K Chase * Taisha
Cullum * Tamara Moore * Tammy
Castleberry * Tammy Lynn Wood * Ted
Murphy * Terri Atkins * Terri Creech * Terry
Raab * Theresa Miracle Harmon * Tonia
Rachael Riggs-Williams * Tonya Mann *
Travis Fleury-Lopez * Twyla Gawlas * Val
Brooks * Walt Munsel * Yvonne Isakson *

Thank you to all these wonderful people.

Thank you for purchasing this book. I hope
you enjoy it as much as I enjoyed writing it
for my faithful readers. Please feel free to
email me to tell me what you thought about
my stories. I love hearing from the readers. I
can be reached at
murdernovels@bobmoats.com

Thanks again!